Never Stop Dreaming

Inspiring short stories of unique and wonderful girls about courage, self-confidence, talents and the potential found in all our dreams

Ellen Mills

Special Art Stories

Never Stop Dreaming

Inspiring short stories of unique and wonderful girls about courage, self-confidence, talent and the potential found in all our dreams

Ellen Mills

PAPERBACK ISBN: 979-12-80592-05-7

support@specialartbooks.com
www.specialartbooks.com

Table of Contents

Introduction

> "Every great dream begins with a dreamer. Always remember, you have within you the strength, the patience, and the passion to reach for the stars and change the world."
>
> — *Harriet Tubman*

Hello, little dreamer.

What's the most incredible dream you've ever had?

Was it about becoming a superhero who could save the world from danger? Maybe you've dreamed about being a wizard who could create anything she wanted with just a flick of her wand. It's wonderful to have such magical dreams while you sleep!

But what kind of dreams do you have when you're awake? Do you dream about doing well at school? Have you dreamed about finding a best friend? Have you dreamed of standing on a stage in front of a crowd without feeling any fear at all? Not everyone's dreams are the same, but one thing is certain: we all have dreams!

Within this book, you will find stories of girls who had dreams of their own. Some of them lived in a world that you might recognize, while others lived in enchanted worlds you've never seen before! Despite these differences, you'll be able to see how all of these girls, despite the difficulties they faced along the way, made their dreams come true.

No dream is too big to be realized. If you believe in yourself and all of the talents and abilities that make you unique, you will have every opportunity to achieve your goals. Don't limit yourself, little dreamer, because a special and wonderful girl like you has all the things she needs to make her dreams come true.

Now, let's start this journey of ours, traveling off to places where fairies, pirates, mermaids, and princesses will find their dreams realized. If you look closely enough, you might see that even in the most magical of words, these girls' dreams might look a little like yours.

A Mermaid's Dream

Have you ever dreamt that you were a mermaid swimming through the deep sea? You could see amazing things and meet wonderful creatures that no one else had ever discovered. Have you ever wanted to do something that no one else thought you could do? Did they ever tell you that you were too small, or that you couldn't be a fighter? That's how Nina the mermaid felt. But like you, young dreamer, she was ready to prove them wrong and make a new friend along the way!

Nina was a mermaid who wanted to be a warrior. She wanted to prove that mermaids could fight, just like the mermen could. None of the mermaids approved; many thought it wasn't ladylike to pick up a sword or a staff.

"Why don't you learn how to sing?" one friend would ask.

"Why don't you learn how to sculpt?" another suggested.

Nina's answer was the same every time: "because I want to learn how to fight! I want to learn how to protect everyone, big and small!" Nina declared.

The others thought she was too small or tried to tell her that the warriors of their cove already protected them well enough. But Nina didn't listen. She would explore the sea, looking for anything that looked like a sword, and sneak over to the warriors' grounds. There, she would watch them closely and try her best to mimic their movements. She did this every day.

However, one day her mother caught her practicing. She shook her head angrily and brought her home. When they got there, her mother insisted that it wasn't safe to sneak around the warriors' grounds, as she could get in trouble.

"Why don't you *ask* to join them, Nina?" her mother suggested.

"I tried. They wouldn't let me train with them," Nina said with a frown.

"Oh, I'm sorry, sweetie. But don't give up. I *know* you can be a great warrior, and they'll see that one day. But until then, I don't want you sneaking around the cove, okay? You need to stay out of trouble."

Nina agreed; nobody else supported her like her mother. Discouraged, she left the next morning without a word and went to a quiet part of the cove where she could sulk in peace.

While she looked down at the darkness below, she thought she could hear a whale crying in the distance. Curious, she swam deeper; the sounds grew louder. She gasped and, without a moment of hesitation, she dove down into the dark water. She swam for some time until she finally found the whale caught under a fishing net.

She rushed to free it, but a shark swam her way.

"Not so fast," he growled, "this whale is my dinner."

Nina froze; she didn't know what to do. Should she run? Should she fight?

The whale shouted: "help me! I don't want to be food!"

Nina looked around and spotted a pole, deep in the bottom of the sea. I know what you're probably thinking—she had to be *really* scared! And you're right, she was. However, she focused on all of her dreams of being a hero instead of focusing on her fear. She swam toward the pole with great speed and used all of her strength to pull it out of the ocean floor. She swam to the shark, showing off her pole, and declared, "I'll protect this whale with all of my might!"

The shark charged towards her, but she stood strong! She swam to the side to avoid it and whacked the shark on the nose as hard as she could.

The shark yelped and swam away, holding its nose.

"You'll pay for this!" The shark said as it swam away.

Nina watched him swim away before safely taking the net off of the whale.

"Thank you for saving me," said the whale, swimming happily in a circle. "My name is Blue."

"I'm Nina. Are you okay?"

"I am now! You're a hero!" Blue cheered.

"I'm glad *you* think so," Nina sighed, her shoulders slumping.

She told Blue about how badly she wanted to be a warrior, and about the other mermaid and mermen's beliefs that she wasn't strong enough.

As they swam up from the dark, Blue shook her head at her. "Nina, you are the bravest mermaid I've ever seen. They would be crazy not to let you be a warrior."

That made Nina smile. Maybe she *could* be strong, just like the warriors in her cove.

“Come on, I want to show you something,” said Blue. Nina followed Blue around the edge of the cove until they came to a small cave. Blue swam into the cave and came out holding an old bronze staff. She gave it to Nina, who excitedly took it into her hands.

“This is for you. I don't want you to give up on your dream. If you want, you can keep it here and practice whenever you want.”

Nina hugged Blue and thanked her for her kindness. Finally, someone else believed in Nina and supported her!

Over the next few days, Nina snuck over to the warriors' cove, as usual, watching the warriors practice. This time, she chose a new hiding spot so that her mother wouldn't find her. After she memorized their movements, she swam to Blue's cave and showed Blue exactly what she learned with her staff. Anytime Nina visited, Blue was excited to see her.

Nina and Blue also explored the cove together and found beautiful things, such as glowing algae and bright pearls hidden in tiny caves behind seaweed.

One day, while Nina was leaving to visit Blue, her mother stopped her.

"Where are you going?" she asked.

"I'm going to visit my best friend, mom!" Nina answered.

Her mother shook her head. "I'm sorry, honey, but you can't go out today. The warriors have been knocking on everyone's doors and telling us that sharks are swimming around the cove, so we have to stay inside."

Nina gasped—she couldn't believe it! She went to the window, and sure enough, sharks circled threateningly through her home, looking for their next dinner. Here and there, warriors clashed with the sharks, their swords or their staffs held high, but there were many more sharks than there were warriors.

"I *have* to go," said Nina.

"I'm sorry, Nina, but you can't; it's not safe. Just go to your room and wait until the sharks leave the cove," her mother insisted.

Nina obeyed her mother and went to her room. What could she do? She didn't even have her staff. She looked out her window, hoping to spot another shark or warrior. However, to her surprise, she spotted a young mermaid hiding in the seaweed nearby. A large shark lurked nearby, and Nina could tell the mermaid was doing her best to escape its attention.

Nina couldn't just sit by and *watch* anymore!

She unlatched her window and carefully slipped out, swimming silently into a patch of seaweed near her house. She quietly made her way to the little girl.

Once the little girl noticed her, she jumped a little, scared by her sudden appearance.

"I'm going to help you, just stay calm," Nina whispered.

The little girl nodded wordlessly and Nina took her hand, leading her through the thick patches of kelp and seaweed until they reached Blue's cave.

"How did you get trapped out there?" Nina asked.

The girl shivered. "I was out playing with my friends when the sharks showed up," she explained. "I think my friends are all still hiding out there. There's ten of us."

Nina nodded; she knew she had to go back for the rest of them. She quietly called for Blue.

Blue swam out to meet them. By the look on her face, Nina knew that Blue could tell something was wrong.

"Blue, the cove is filled with sharks. I need you to watch over her while I try to find her friends, and I need my staff," said Nina.

Blue nodded and gave Nina her staff. She patted the young girl on the shoulder with her fin. "You can count on me!" said Blue.

And she was right; Nina knew she could count on her. As Nina slipped through the vines, she found other young mermaids hiding behind buildings or in large patches of seaweed. Each time she went into the cove, her heart raced, fear filling her chest. However, when she saw a child in need, all of the fear faded and bravery emerged. They all told her the same story; one moment, they'd been playing a game, and the next they were all swimming as fast as they could for cover. She snuck the lonesome children back to Blue one by one, reuniting them with their friends. While some children were easy to sneak to Blue, others were not.

"Not so fast!" one shark said. Nina quickly hid the young mermaid in the patch of seaweed behind her before holding her staff up, just like the warriors did. The shark dove after her, and just like last time, she swam out of the way and hit it really hard on the nose with her staff. The shark shrunk back and swam away.

By the end of the day, Nina had saved all ten children. They spent the day quietly playing games and telling stories in Blue's cave until they heard a cheer from the cove. Nina peeked out of Blue's cave and saw the warriors celebrating together; they had scared all of the sharks away! Nina told all of the other children the good news and they returned to the cove together.

As they were reunited with their parents, they cheered Nina's name!

"Nina kept us safe!" said one.

"Nina fought the sharks!" said another.

Everyone in the cove was shocked and thanked Nina for keeping their loved ones safe. Her mother hugged her tight, saying that she was very scared to notice her gone but happy that she was safe.

The leader of the warriors swam up to her with a smile. "Thank you for your bravery, Miss Nina," he said. "It is with great respect that I would like to make you one of our warriors."

Nina excitedly accepted, of course. She later trained side by side with the warriors that she had once watched from afar, and every time she did, she returned to Blue's cave to tell her what she'd learned.

Did you know that you could be a warrior, too, little dreamer? You could learn how to keep others safe just like Nina. It takes a great amount of courage, but that courage is within you! It's okay to be scared, just as Nina was. When you focus on making a change instead of focusing on your fear, you too can become a warrior.

A Pirate Party

Have you ever dreamt of adventure? If you do, do you see yourself as a pilot? Maybe an astronaut? Well, how's about a pirate? This story begins with a girl named Velma on the day that she became a pirate, just like the rest of her family!

That morning, Velma woke up excited. Why, you may ask? She was excited because it was her birthday, the day she would finally become a full-fledged pirate!

She jumped out of bed and put on her nicest pirate clothes. She tied her bandana around her head and ran up the stairs to the main deck of the ship. She breathed in the salty air and felt herself get even more excited.

“Good morning, Velma! Are you ready for today?” her mother asked.

“Of course! I’m ready for anything!” Velma insisted, bouncing around the main deck.

“That’s good because we have a *special* mission today. Come with me down to the kitchen,” her mother said, taking her hand.

They went down to the kitchen together, where her father was cooking pancakes. He gave her a heaping plate and she ate them happily. While she ate, her father unrolled a large map, covering most of the table. He told Velma all about the journey he'd planned, explaining that it might be dangerous. Velma listened closely; the mission would require passing Skull Cove, sneaking through the Kraken Sea, and landing on the Island of Mystery, where they would look for a secret treasure.

Velma was very excited but also very nervous, as she wanted to prove herself to her family. She nodded her head in understanding and the family hit the seas!

Their first stop was Skull Cove, which was filled with skeletons looking for a fight. Velma was excited when her mom handed her a sword, but when they arrived and skeletons began to climb into the ship, Velma got scared. She was starting to shake when she felt her father's hand on her shoulder and looked back at both of her parents. They nodded at her confidently and let her know that she had their support! Velma nodded back, feeling reassured, and she kept her sword straight to prepare for battle.

After a lot of tricky sword-fighting, she defeated all of the skeletons! Her parents patted her on the back and told her how proud they were of her.

Their next stop was the Kraken Sea. To get through this, she had to navigate their ship carefully so that they didn't wake the Kraken. Just like her parents taught her, she pulled the sails gently, careful not to be too loud. Her father told her she was doing a wonderful job and encouraged her to continue. However, just as they thought all was well, Velma accidentally slipped and pushed the sails too far. The wood holding the sails made a loud creaking noise, which sounded even louder than usual because of how quiet they had been. Suddenly, the water around their boat became rough and choppy, causing their boat to sway side to side, and the loud, deep call of the Kraken echoed from deep below the water.

Velma was so scared that she didn't know what to do, so she let go of the wheel and turned to her mom. "What do we do?" Velma asked.

Her mother kneeled next to her and put a hand on her shoulder. "You know what to do," she insisted. "Just think like a pirate!"

After a moment of thinking, Velma remembered her old violin back in her cabin. She ran to get the fiddle before rushing back out and standing on the deck.

The Kraken emerged from the water, yelling angrily. Velma gulped and began to play the fiddle very carefully, trying to calm it down with a nice and sweet lullaby. As she played, the Kraken calmed down and slowly began to swim back down to the bottom of the sea. Before long, she heard the deep sound of the Kraken snoring on the seafloor and she set the violin down, sighing in relief.

"Good job, Velma!" her mother said. "It's time for the final destination, the Island of Mystery."

After a bit of navigation, the family landed on the Island of Mystery. It's said that the island plays tricks on those who set foot on its sand and makes them see things that aren't there. As Velma stepped down onto the beach, she looked around, noticing that there were bright red spots just off in the distance.

"What do you see, Velma?" asked her father.

"I see a lot of marks, but I'm not quite sure what they are," she said.

"Well, let's go check it out then," suggested her mother.

Her parents stepped onto the beach behind her and they walked down the shore together. Velma couldn't believe her eyes as she approached the red marks; the island was covered in red X's!

"Mom, Dad, look!" Velma said, pointing. "X marks the spot! There's so much treasure here!"

Velma's mother gave her a shovel and let her look around carefully. She chose the nearest X and began to dig into the sand, only to realize that there was nothing there. The island had played a trick on her! She tried another X, and then another, but none of them had treasure! She felt discouraged, but her parents encouraged her to continue.

"Don't give up, Velma. You just have to focus," her father said.

Velma held her head up high and looked around, focusing on the details of the landscape. She looked off to her left and thought she saw another red X, but when she ran towards it, she realized it was a bright red V.

Confused but determined, Velma dug in until her shovel hit something hard under the sand with a large *clunk*.

"I did it! I found something!" Velma exclaimed.

Her parents came over and helped her lift the giant treasure chest out of the sand.

"You did a great job!" her mother cheered.

"Yeah, now open that up and claim what's yours," her father added.

Velma reached for the latch but stopped. She didn't *want* to open it.

Some might find this crazy—after all, she'd been working for it all day!—but she had a reason, young dreamer.

"Is something wrong?" asked her father.

"Well, I enjoyed today so much that I don't really *care* that I found a treasure chest. In fact, I think we should open it together. You guys earned it, too," Velma said with a smile.

"Alright then, if you think we should open it, then we'll open it together," said her mother. The family pushed the heavy lid up and found a bunch of gold coins and a note.

Velma took the note and read it carefully.

Dear Velma,

Happy birthday!

Love, your mom and dad.

Velma was so happy that she was about to cry. Her parents helped her find a chest of *gold* for her birthday.

Remember, young dreamer: when you reach your destination, don't forget about the journey you took to get there. When you try to reach your dreams, remember what you did along the way. Did you fight skeletons? Did you practice doing the things you love to do? Maybe you even helped your loved ones win a game and had fun doing it. Remember to have fun along the way and enjoy the process, especially with your family.

A Princess in Search of Friends

Have you ever felt alone in the world? Do you worry you're not good enough to make a friend? Guess what, little dreamer, that's not true! And princess Annabelle will prove it.

Princess Annabelle was a very busy girl. She had many tasks each day, as she was part of the royal court. In the mornings, she practiced her posture by walking with a book on her head. In the afternoon, she took classes on how to be a proper princess and make decrees. In the evening, she ate with her family and talked about her day before taking a bath and going to bed.

You would *think* that Annabelle was happy. She had the most beautiful dresses and crowns, she could have any toy that she wanted, and she could easily request the greatest of sweets at her request. However, she didn't care about those things. Being busy didn't spare her a lot of time to run around and play, and it's hard to care about toys and sweets when you feel lonely. The only things she *truly* wanted were to be a normal girl and to have a friend.

Little did she know, her wish would come true.

One day, one of her maids brought her daughter to work with her. "Please forgive me, Princess," she begged, "I had to bring my daughter with me today because my husband is sick. We'll be headed into town soon to pick up some supplies." She bowed deeply.

"That's okay, don't worry about it," Annabelle said. She looked behind the maid to see a girl her age peeking out from behind her mother. "Hi, what's your name?" Annabelle asked.

The girl seemed shy, but she slowly stepped closer. "My name is Tilda, Princess," she answered nervously.

Annabelle held out her hand and Tilda carefully shook it.

"This may sound kind of weird, but could I go into town with you two today?" Annabelle asked the maid shyly.

Tilda's face filled with excitement. "Oh, can she, mother? Please?" Tilda asked the maid.

The maid tentatively nodded, saying that she could as long as they got the King and Queen's permission. Annabelle asked her parents and they agreed, thinking it would be a good lesson for her to know her people.

The girls were excited, and Annabelle was given some clothes provided by the maids so she could blend in.

"You look wonderful, Your Highness," Tilda said.

"You can call me Annabelle," the princess said shyly.

"Okay," Tilda said with a smile.

The three went into town with guards, all of them disguised as regular people. One of the guards walked close behind them and answered any questions Annabelle had that Tilda couldn't answer.

"This is exciting. I've never been outside of the castle walls before," Annabelle whispered.

"Do you at least get to play with your friends?" asked Tilda.

"I... I don't really have any," Annabelle admitted, her shoulders falling.

"That's crazy! Everyone has a friend," Tilda insisted.

"I'm not one of them, I'm afraid."

"But what if you *are*? I mean, *I'll* be your friend," Tilda offered.

"You don't really know me," Annabelle pointed out with a grin.

"But I can try to. You seem nice, and I bet you're really fun!" Tilda insisted, nudging Annabelle's arm.

Annabelle smiled, excitement filling her. “I’m glad you think so.”

As they continued to walk through the street, a little girl ran by them and Annabelle felt something touch her wrist. When she looked, her bracelet was gone! Where did it go? Annabelle looked around frantically and saw the girl that ran by, clutching the bracelet in her hand.

“Wait! That’s mine!” Annabelle yelled, running after her. Tilda followed, and the two chased after the girl down several streets as their guards tried to keep up. Before long, their guards caught the girl. As Annabelle and Tilda drew closer, they saw that the little girl was clutching the bracelet with tears falling from her eyes.

“Your highness, we caught the thief. How will you punish her?” asked one of the guards.

Annabelle looked at the crying little girl and shook her head. “Just let her go,” she said. The guards slowly put her down, and the girl immediately held the bracelet out to her.

"Why did you steal my bracelet?" the princess asked calmly.

"I... I thought if I sold it, I could help feed my family," the girl sniffled.

Annabelle slowly pushed the bracelet towards the girl and gave her the pocket money that her parents had given her.

"Take this to feed your family," she insisted.

The little girl thanked her greatly and ran towards her home.

"Why did you do that?" asked Tilda.

"Because I want to rule with kindness and hope when I take the throne. That kindness will build friendships."

“Honestly, I didn’t think you *would* let her go, especially with your bracelet. You’ll make a great queen one day,” Tilda said with a grin.

As the girls walked back to the castle, Annabelle noticed a group of children playing and watched for a moment. Tilda noticed her watching and took her hand, pulling her towards the other kids so they could join. However, as they reached the kids, the group stopped playing and stared at them instead.

“Uh, hi. My, um... my name is Ann, and I was wondering if we could join in the game you’re playing,” Annabelle asked with a smile.

The children looked at each other and shook their heads. “No, thanks. We saw the guards chase after that other girl, and we don’t want any trouble,” one of them spoke up.

"But that girl stole her bracelet!" Tilda said, but Annabelle took her hand.

"It's fine, Tilda. They said no, so we should leave." Annabelle pulled Tilda away and sat in a corner, away from the other children. Tilda grumbled that they were rude while the princess sulked.

"Maybe I'm not meant to be a normal girl," said the princess.

Tilda sat next to her and hugged her. "You're normal to me," she said.

Annabelle laughed as she wiped her tears away. The girls were laughing together when they were approached by another little girl.

"Um, hi," she said.

The girls looked up and saw that it was the girl that had taken her bracelet.

"Oh, is your family okay?" Annabelle asked immediately, standing up.

"They're fine, I just wanted to thank you for forgiving me. And... And I wanted to say I'm sorry," she said, bowing her head.

"What's your name?" asked Annabelle.

"Eliza," the girl answered.

"Eliza, we were just thinking about a game to play. Do you want to join us?" Annabelle asked with a smile.

Eliza nodded and the trio began to run around, playing different games just like the children that the princess had seen. They were all having so much fun until one of the kids from the other group called out to Eliza.

"Eliza, why are you hanging out with those girls? You know they're not like us," the boy insisted, crossing his arms.

"I'm hanging out with them because they're my friends. They don't judge me, and they're nice," Eliza argued, crossing her arms back.

Annabelle stepped in front of her and put her hand out, surprising them both. "My name is Ann, what's your name?"

The boy took a moment to think before shaking her hand. "I'm Danny," he said.

"Do you want to play with us, Danny?" Annabelle asked with a grin.

"Sure," he agreed.

Annabelle suddenly found herself with many friends, and the more she played, the more kids joined. When she returned on the weekends, the children were excited to see her. She had finally made friends.

Let this be known, young dreamer: everyone deserves love. It doesn't matter if you're rich or poor. If you strive for friends, know that it is always possible. Don't forget to be kind, don't forget to be accepting, and, above all, don't forget to be yourself.

The Dancers

Have you and your friend ever shared the same dream, but only one of you got it? How would you feel? Would you feel happy or sad? Little Grace didn't know how to feel when her friend Nicole got the solo she wanted, so what did Grace do?

Little Grace and Nicole were best friends who dreamed of taking over the world through dance and being professional ballerinas. Their dream was to dance on stage in front of hundreds of people, maybe even thousands! One day, their dance teacher announced that there would be an important solo in their next recital that could determine the choice of others in the future.

"How exciting!" Grace said to Nicole.

"How *scary*," Nicole replied.

"Let's practice together so we can both do well!" said Grace.

Nicole shook her head. "I'm not sure I want to audition. I don't think I'm ready for something this big."

"How would you know if you don't try? Come on! This is the kind of thing we've been dreaming of," Grace insisted, taking her hands and spinning around with her.

The girls giggled and Nicole half-heartedly agreed to try out.

They stayed later after class to practice. Nicole felt herself make many mistakes, while Grace felt confident in her steps. When the day came, Nicole and Grace auditioned for the solo.

As Grace performed her audition, she took deep breaths with every spin. She kept her arms in the correct positions and made sure that every step was done with precision. When she finished, she felt nervous, but overall she was confident that she would get it. She took her seat and watched as Nicole came on the stage.

When the music played, Nicole was frozen. She wasn't moving at all! The teacher stopped the music and stepped up to Nicole, whispering a few words of encouragement. When the dancer nodded her head, the teacher sat back down and played the music again. This time, Nicole looked at

Grace who was giving her a thumbs up for encouragement. Nicole grinned and took a deep breath. She began to dance with a passion Grace had never seen before. Though Nicole missed a step or two, she didn't let it phase her as she continued to spin with as much grace as she could.

The teacher said that the girls both did very well, but since Nicole performed just a little better, she would get the solo.

Grace was shocked. She had been so confident that she would get it, so she felt very upset that she didn't get chosen. She felt the tears run down her face and ran out of the studio, feeling heartbroken. She didn't go back inside that day and waited for her mother to pick her up outside.

When her mom arrived, she asked what was wrong immediately.

"Nicole got the solo and I didn't," Grace said sadly.

"Did you congratulate her?"

Grace thought for a moment and realized that she didn't. Now she felt even worse. "What do I do? I want to be happy for Nicole, but I'm also really sad that I didn't get the part."

Grace was lost, but her mother shook her head. "It's fine to be upset when you don't get the part, but you can't forget to be happy for those who did get it. You can be both at the same time. Tomorrow, I want you to be honest with Nicole and let her know you are there for her. Don't let this one solo mess up your friendship."

"You're right," Grace nodded.

And the next day, she did just that. She approached Nicole and gave her a big hug. "I'm sorry, Nicole. I was so upset that I didn't consider your feelings. Congratulations on the solo. I know you'll do well!" Grace smiled.

Nicole smiled but kept her head down. "I'm not sure I want the part. I don't think I'm that good, and I know I make a lot of mistakes."

"That's crazy! You're very talented, and I know you can do it. I'll even practice with you the whole way so we can both get better!" Grace said.

Nicole smiled; she felt better knowing that her friend had her back.

Each day, the girls stayed late to practice and made comments on what they could both work on. Sometimes the comments were taken with understanding, and sometimes they were taken with frustration. The closer they got to the recital, the more mistakes Nicole made.

"You have to stay steady," Grace said.

"I'm trying," Nicole huffed. She tried to spin again, but lost her footing and fell.

When Grace went to see if she was okay, she saw the tears in her best friend's eyes. She knelt and asked what was wrong.

"Don't you get it? I'm not as talented as you!" Nicole cried. "I make so many more mistakes and I'm going to mess up out there," she said, putting her head in her hands. "Maybe I can talk to the teacher and she'll let you perform."

Did you hear that? Nicole is willing to give Grace the solo she wanted! You might think that Grace would take this offer, but instead, she sat next to her friend and patted her back.

"No way. There's a reason you were chosen for this solo. The teacher wouldn't think differently. You can do this. Just believe in yourself; I believe in you," Grace said with a grin. She stood up and pulled Nicole to her feet. "I'll be right by you, no matter what!"

Nicole wiped her tears away and her face changed to one of determination. “Okay, I can do this.” She hugged Grace tightly and said, “You know, the only reason I’ve done so well is that I had you by my side. If you weren’t there, I don’t think I would have ever made it this far.”

Grace laughed. “You always had the passion, and I’ll be there to push you through!”

The girls continued to practice, and Nicole was slowly perfecting her part. As the two practiced the solo each day, their teacher sometimes stayed later to help them as well. Just three days before the recital, she held Grace and Nicole back to share some good news.

“I’ve watched how well you two have grown together and am pleased to announce that I want you both to perform the solo!” their teacher grinned.

Grace and Nicole were surprised and hugged each other happily. When the recital came, the two danced together beautifully and continued to support each other. It went much better than either of them expected, and even their teacher was very surprised and proud of their performance.

Have you ever felt like Grace? It's okay to feel sad when you don't reach your dream when you want to, but don't forget to support those who did. When you support others in their dreams, you'll grow even stronger in achieving your own.

To Touch the Sky

I hope you have big dreams, young dreamer. It's wonderful to have set your goals way up high, but have you ever become frustrated while trying to reach them? Have you ever felt like no matter what you did, your goals were out of reach? Lilly would know how you feel, as her dream was to fly, like all of the other fairies.

Lilly, unlike most fairies, was born without wings. Because of this, she was unable to fly like everyone else. You would think she would sulk every day about watching her friends zip through the sky, but she didn't. Instead, she was ready to do whatever she could to join them in the air.

Even though Lilly didn't have wings, she was very creative and always willing to learn. One of the first things she did was learn about tools, even asking her mother if she could have a workshop. Her mother agreed, but only if she used her tools safely and wore protective gear, such as safety goggles and a helmet, so that she wouldn't get hurt. Lilly spent days and nights learning how to use all of her tools correctly and even read many books to get an idea of what she could invent. When she had an idea, she was ready to begin her journey into the creative unknown. She built many inventions. Each of them would fail many times, but she refused to give up.

One day, she asked her friend to join her in the workshop so she could trace her wings. As she traced, she admitted; "I want to fly like everyone else, but I'm not sure where to start."

"I don't see why you're so focused on flying," her friend said, holding as still as she could. "You know we love you just the way you are."

"I know you do, but this feels like something bigger. I want to touch the sky! I want to feel what you guys feel every day when you're in the air," explained Lilly.

When she finished sketching out the wings, she let her friend step aside and she grabbed her tools. After her friend left, she got to work making a set of wings that would not only work but also look beautiful. When she finished her first version, she tried them on and activated them. She was able to lift off the ground to a tall height and glide down smoothly, but she couldn't stay in the air. She tried again and again, adjusting the wings little by little, but they simply wouldn't work.

"This won't do," Lilly grumbled, shaking her head. She tossed her wings to the side. It didn't go as she hoped, but she wasn't discouraged; she was ready to start the next experiment from scratch. Her next approach was to make fairy dust. She mixed a few chemicals, trying to recreate the magical properties of the dust. This also took a few tries—the first version made her sneeze a lot, the second mixture made her mouth taste like vegetables for hours, and the third turned her hair and tongue green! Finally, on the fourth try, she was able to make dust that would lift her off the ground. Did she do it? Did she succeed? Unfortunately, no. She was able to stay afloat, but not very high off the ground. She was also able to move in every direction but up. When she came back to the ground, she stored it in the cupboard with a big sigh. If flying didn't work out, maybe she could go into the candy-making business. Although "long-lasting vegetable flavor" probably wouldn't be very popular...

"At least my tongue isn't green," she shrugged. She tried to look on the bright side, but she was slowly giving up. Maybe she didn't *have* to have wings or look like a fairy. At this point, as long as she got to the sky, she could at least accomplish *something* towards her goal of flying.

Her third attempt was to make rocket boots that could lift her and keep her afloat. She added fuel so that she'd be able to race with some of the other fairies. When she finished and tried them on, she was getting high up in the air! She did it—she was flying! However, she couldn't steer or go anywhere. She was stuck in one place. That is, until the rockets malfunctioned; before long, she was spinning out of control, and she couldn't steer at all!

"Oh no, oh no, oh no! I'm going to crash!" she yelled. She braced herself as she twirled towards the ground, tumbling into a pile of leaves. She laid there for a moment, groaning, as her boots ran out of fuel and finally sputtered to a stop. She sat up, took off her boots, and threw them into a pile with her wings.

After that, she went inside and stayed in her room until her mother called her for dinner. When she came to the table, her mother sat a plate of sweet nectar in front of her.

“How are your experiments going?” She asked.

“Terrible. No matter what I do, I just can’t get to the sky! I’ve worked on this all day, and nothing works!” Lilly sighed. “I’m never gonna fly. I’ll just be stuck down here.”

“I know you’re more stubborn than that,” her mom said with a grin. “Maybe you should take a break for the day. Sometimes, we work so hard towards something that we don't see the big picture. So, after dinner, get some rest and go back to your workshop tomorrow with a fresh mind," her mother suggested.

"I guess that could work," Lilly shrugged. "I don't have another option. What could go wrong at this point?"

She did as her mom told her and went to bed, feeling more tired than she had realized. When she returned to the workshop the next day, she stood back and looked at what she had made so far. One made her jump high and float down smoothly. One made her float and control her direction, but it couldn't reach the height of the sky. The last let her reach the sky, but wouldn't let her go anywhere, and could malfunction.

Lilly thought hard for a moment as she looked at her work and realized, what if she put them all together? So she did.

She put on her wings, dabbed the fairy dust onto her shoulders, and pulled her boots on. She ran outside and activated them all; she glided easily to the sky, and was able to control her flying! When her friends spotted her, they joined her in case anything went wrong, but nothing did! She'd done it! When she came to the ground, she floated down safely with ease.

Now, she could feel the sky.

She asked her friends to stay with her as she got ready to fly higher. She took a deep breath and flew up just as she did before, but this time she kept going and going, watching her home and workshop shrink to tiny dots below her.

"You're really flying Lilly! You did it!" her friends cheered.

"Yeah," Lilly smiled, soaring through the air. "I really am."

Sometimes we need to take a step back from our work and revisit it with fresh eyes, young dreamer. If we focus too hard, we may miss what is right in front of us. So when you focus on your dream, try not to get too caught up in the tiny details; look back at the path you made to get there. Some failures can turn into successes in the end.

Cookies for Santa

Have you ever dreamt of winning a competition, but you weren't sure what to do? Did you ever make many projects, but not know which would be the best to turn in? A little elf named Lucy had this very same problem when she entered a baking contest. However, this wasn't just *any* baking contest—this contest was to see who could make the best cookies for Santa.

Little Lucy wanted to become the best baker in all of the North Pole so she could make Santa the best cookies imaginable, and she was so excited when she heard he would be holding a baking competition. The winner would be the best baker in the North Pole! Lucy was very excited, but also very nervous. She had to make the perfect recipe!

While Lucy was baking, her mother came into the kitchen, looking confused by all of the different ingredients around the kitchen. "Are you making cookies?" she asked.

"I am. I have to make the best recipe so Santa will pick mine," said Lucy. She was already stirring three different doughs together, and her clothes were covered in flour.

"Why don't you make your famous chocolate chip cookies? I remember those were amazing, maybe even the best I'd ever had," her mother suggested.

"I can't make chocolate chip cookies, mom! That's what everyone *else* will make. I have to make something that stands out. I can't make something that plain and boring."

"I still think those would be a definite winner, but I'll be cheering you on no matter what," her mother said with a smile.

Lucy continued to work hard, and over time, she ended up with several batches of cookies. She had snickerdoodles, sugar cookies, and peanut butter cookies with hints of cinnamon, but as she gave herself more and more options, she couldn't decide which she wanted to enter. They all tasted really good, but they could also be so much *better*. The more she focused on what to bake, the sadder and sadder she got. Her gut was telling her that something wasn't right.

On the day of the competition, each elf lined up in the kitchen of Santa's workshop, the timer set and their workstations stocked with all of the ingredients they could need.

At the center of it all, Santa Clause stood, shaking with jolly laughter before he began to speak. "Ho, ho, ho! Thank you all for joining us as we watch our fellow elves bake some of the best cookies! Now, we do have some rules, but they're very simple: first, you can bake as many cookies as you want within the time limit, but only one batch should be submitted. Second, you need to stay safe when you bake. And third, the biggest rule of all, have fun! Now, let's begin!"

The elves cheered and Lucy and her rivals went to work. She tied her apron tight and focused on her work, baking more and more batches. However, when she tried the cookies, none of them tasted *right*. It's not that they tasted terrible, it's just that they didn't taste as great as they could have.

She was beginning to get more and more frustrated with each batch, and she almost wanted to quit.

When she gazed over at the other elves, she became even more worried; so many of them had confident faces! Many of their cookies were amazingly decorative, topped with fun-tasting glitter and cut into different shapes, like reindeer and mistletoe.

When she looked back at her own cookies, her shoulders slumped.

She glanced at the clock and gasped. "Oh no, I'm running out of time!" she exclaimed. She quickly counted out her ingredients and realized that she didn't have much to work with. As she dug deeper through them, she realized she had just enough to make her chocolate chip cookies. She sighed and began mixing. However, this time, something felt different. She was beginning to feel... happy. It was as if all of the memories of when she baked before flooded back to her. She remembered the first time she made her mother's recipe, the first time she added her personal touch to them, and the first time she gave them to her mom and watched her smile after the first bite. Everything she did to make them special for others gave her the joy to make them again.

As she spooned the dough onto the pan, she was smiling more and more. When she slid them into the oven, she suddenly felt her confidence returning.

The oven dinged and she took the cookies out, proud of what she had accomplished. They looked like regular chocolate chip cookies, but she felt a great sense of joy in the

finished batch. She noticed some of the other elves in the stands commenting on how good they smelled. She then poured a glass of milk and waited patiently.

The timer buzzed and everyone put down their tools. Santa made his rounds, tasting the cookies at each stand and making comments.

"These glitter cookies look amazing, but they do seem to be a little burnt at the bottom," he said. He then went to another stand and laughed at the reindeer-shaped cookies. He tried them with milk and smiled, "The reindeer cookies taste wonderful, but they don't seem to mix too well with the milk. They are quite creative though!"

He then moved on to Lucy. She rubbed her hands together as she was very anxious.

"These cookies smell fantastic!" Santa announced. He took one bite of the cookies and his face pinched up oddly. Lucy felt herself shake with anticipation, as it was not the reaction she was expecting.

“This is an... interesting flavor,” said Santa.

Lucy waited for him to call out her defeat when he gave a hardy laugh.

“I don’t think I’ve tasted cookies this well made in centuries! I think we have a winner!”

Lucy’s heart raced as the crowd cheered. Santa leaned in so that she could hear him and chuckled, “Do you know why you are the winner?” he asked.

“Um... is it because of the cookies?” she laughed nervously.

“That is a big reason, yes. But I chose you because many forgot my last rule. They forgot to have fun. All of the elves were so focused on the competition and worried so much about how the cookies *looked*. But when I saw your table, you were smiling and taking your time, like you were enjoying yourself.”

"The truth is, Santa... I wasn't really having fun at the start," Lucy admitted.

"So what changed?" Santa asked, his face puzzled.

"I don't know. I think it was because of the chocolate chip cookies. I truly love making them. I was just worried they wouldn't stand out," she shrugged.

"Well, they definitely did. In fact," he turned to the crowd. "I think I will crown this batch as this year's best cookies in all of the North Pole!"

The crowd cheered even louder as he poured a glass of milk and handed it to Lucy. Lucy took it carefully and he held his glass to her.

"Cheers, little Lucy," he smiled. The two clinked glasses and ate her cookies together.

Did you find the message, young dreamer? Don't forget to have fun while you achieve your dreams. Remember to smile and laugh as you work hard towards your goals. If you don't have fun, you might end up with some burnt cookies.

The Dog Who Was Loved

There may be a time where you have to look at two things that matter to you and choose what is more important. You may want to do one thing, but something else popped up and you weren't able to do what you originally wanted to. Maybe you had to make a hard decision and put your wants aside. Isabell knew this all too well when a dog show came to town.

Isabell loved animals and wanted to be a veterinarian, just like her mother. Sometimes, she came with her mother to the animal hospital and helped with small things, such as giving the animals treats after their appointments and learning about how to take care of them when they were sick. If the animal was hurt, she learned how to wrap up their legs and would even give them words of encouragement so that they wouldn't feel so scared. She saw many types of animals, from dogs and cats to bunnies and gerbils! It was very exciting, but at the end of the day, she had someone special waiting at home. When she was at home, she had her own dog that she loved very much, and her name was Sofia.

Isabell wanted to give Sofia the best care possible. She brushed her almost every day, walked her several times a day, and was even careful with the food she ate. She made sure to show Sofia as much affection as she could, and she trained her with simple commands so her dog would listen to her carefully.

One day, a dog show was coming to town, and Isabell was very excited. They had a junior league and an adult league. In the junior league, she would have to show that their dog had good grooming standards, could perform a few basic commands, and could run a simple obstacle course.

"You hear that, Sofia? There's a dog show coming to our little town! I know if we entered, we would win!" Isabell smiled. Sofia barked excitedly, as though she agreed.

"Let's practice for the show. I bet the more we do, the better our chances will be!"

And so Isabell and Sofia practiced everything for the dog show in their backyard. First, Isabell started by checking Sofia's grooming and made especially sure that she was getting brushed regularly.

Next, they would practice simple commands such as sit, lay down, and shake. They even started practicing some jumping tricks, in case the judges wanted to see more.

And last, they would practice an obstacle course that her mother had helped her make with a few wooden stands and a plastic tunnel. Isabell timed Sofia's run but made sure she wasn't tiring her out.

Everything was looking fantastic. That is, until the night before the show, when Sofia got sick.

"Mom, I don't think Sofia is okay," said Isabell. Whenever she pet Sofia, her dog looked at her and whined. Her mother looked at her and felt around her stomach.

"Oh sweetie, I think she has a tummy ache. We may need to take her to the vet tomorrow so we can get some X-rays."

"But we can't do that, the dog show is tomorrow!" Isabell pleaded.

"Well, part of being a veterinarian is making the right call for your animals. So what do you think we should do?" her mother asked.

Isabell thought for a moment. On the one hand, they had trained hard for the dog show, and she wanted to show the town how amazing Sofia was. On the other, she knew Sofia wasn't feeling well and was worried she would feel worse if she didn't get help soon. At first, it seemed a little hard to choose. But when she thought of what was important, she made her choice.

"I think we should get Sofia to the vet. She's not feeling well, and I don't want her to feel worse," said Isabell. Her mother nodded her head. The next morning, they all went to the vet together. Sofia got some X-rays, and Isabell and her mom found out that her dog needed antibiotics for her stomach ache.

When they got home, Isabell took out some cheese and gave Sofia her medicine, then sat on the couch with her dog and stayed with her all night, waiting for her to get better. Soon, Isabell fell asleep next to her Sofia and woke up the next morning to see Sofia a lot happier. She was excited to go outside and was drinking water normally.

Isabell looked at the time and noticed that the dog show was already over. She turned on the TV just in time to see that they had announced the winner for the children's league. She felt sad for a moment but realized that Sofia would have felt worse if she had performed.

"You know girl, I don't need to show them that you're the best dog ever, because I already know that you are," Isabell said, petting her dog's head.

Her mother came in to check on them and was happy to see both were doing well. "Someone is looking better," she said, patting Sofia on the head. She sat on the couch next to her daughter and looked at the TV.

"I know you wanted to compete, but I think you did the right thing. You put Sofia's health before your wants, and I'm so proud of you for that. You're going to be a wonderful vet one day," her mother said with a smile.

"Thanks, Mom. Honestly, I'm really glad I got her help. And besides, when the dog show comes next year, we'll be ready!" Isabell said with a grin. Sofia barked in agreement. That day, the two continued to train, and Isabell continued to give her dog all of the love in the world.

The moral of this story, young dreamer, is to take care of the ones you love. It could be your friends, your family, or even your pets, but watch over them while you achieve your dreams. If they need you, then they need you; opportunities to follow your dreams will always be around the corner.

The Patient Painter

Throughout this book, you have learned about many young girls who have reached their dreams and goals. These girls worked hard to do so, and I hope you do, as well. However, something that isn't often thought about when we pursue our dreams is the time it takes to reach them. Patience is very important, and Emma would be challenged by this.

Emma dreamed of being a painter that was known around the world. She had been painting since she was very young. Her mother took her to a gallery and Emma was surprised at all of the beautiful art around her. Some pieces were photos and some were sculptures, but Emma's favorite parts of the whole gallery were the paintings.

Anytime she looked at the paintings, she felt a light within herself. They inspired her, and she realized that she wanted her work to be displayed in the gallery one day, so she could inspire others in that way. When she got home, she asked her mother if she could have a few art supplies. Her mother agreed.

From there, she set up a little art studio and began to paint canvases to the best of her ability. When she did this, though, she wasn't happy with her work. She felt as though she could do even better. So what could she do to improve her paintings? Emma thought for a while before she had a realization. "If I'm going to be a great artist, I need to learn how!" Emma told herself.

She signed up for lessons at her school and practiced every day until she noticed that her work was slowly improving. Once she felt confident enough, she went to the art gallery and asked to submit her paintings.

The woman at the desk smiled but shook her head. "I appreciate you taking an interest in our gallery. Unfortunately, we're not taking submissions right now. Maybe if you improve, you can try again next year," she smiled.

Emma was disappointed but she refused to give up. She went to more classes and continued her work. She was even getting more praise from her teachers as her art slowly grew into the work she dreamed of creating. She waited a year and returned to the gallery, this time with newer and better pieces to present. The woman was surprised to see a great improvement, but her work was still turned down—Emma couldn't believe it!

"Did you not like my work?" Emma asked.

"Your work is great, but I believe it could be better. So, unfortunately, I won't be taking any of your submissions," the woman said, shaking her head.

Emma went home, feeling very discouraged. She sat in her room and wondered if she would ever reach her dream. She had been working so hard for so long and was still getting rejected. She looked back on all of the lessons she had taken and remembered something.

All of the artists that she had studied had been painting for years before they were recognized, and they didn't give up when they were rejected. In fact, they continued, because they loved making art for the sake of making it, not for the sake of approval. Emma smiled and went back to work. She continued her lessons and even began to put a set of paintings together. One day, as she was almost finished, she stood up to get some towels and accidentally knocked over her canvas and all of her paint spilled over her work.

"Oh no!" she shouted. She picked up the paint before it got worse, but it was too late. The paint had spread all over the canvas. Emma began to cry as the final piece of her work had been ruined. She had worked so hard for all of these years and had kept her head up so many times, and this one canvas made her break down.

When she was done crying, she picked the canvas back up and set it back on the easel. She went to bed and came back the next day and found that the paint never dried, so it ran down the canvas in a dripping multitude of colors.

"Huh," said Emma. "It actually looks kind of... beautiful," she realized. She slowly began to smile. She took the canvas and put it with her other pieces, deciding she would add it to her submissions.

And when another year came, she returned to the art gallery. Oddly enough, she wasn't as confident as she was in prior years.

"Always exciting to see you, Emma. What did you bring this year?" The woman asked with a smile.

"I thought that instead of bringing you a bunch of unrelated pieces, I would bring you a set," Emma said, giving her a nervous smile in return.

"Alright, let's see it!"

Emma took out the pieces and laid them out to show her. The first was a rusted watch that was coated in dirt. In the next painting, the outsides of the watch were polished, but the insides remained unclean. And in the final, the clock was completely clean with a vine of flowers woven around it. And then, the very last was the canvas with run-down colors.

“What’s this one supposed to be?” asked the woman.

“That... is what happens when you mess up from time to time. It looks and feels really bad and messy, but in the end, it can be something beautiful.”

“Well, I think it’s safe to say that you put a lot of thought into your work. I think with these pieces, the gallery will be more than happy to showcase them this year!”

Emma’s heart raced; she had finally made it. She and her mother celebrated with a dinner at her favorite restaurant, and she excitedly waited for the day she would see her art hung up on the walls. As she put on her shoes, her mother came in to do her hair.

"I'm so proud of you, sweetheart," her mother chuckled.

"Because I painted some awesome art?" Emma laughed.

"Because you didn't give up. You were rejected so many times, and you still picked yourself up and stayed with it. You could have quit at any time and even had some messes along the way, but you proved your love and patience for your passion," her mother said with a grin. She finished Emma's hair and took her hand. "Now, let's go see some art."

Emma entered the gallery and found herself in awe when she saw her work on the wall. She almost cried; she had finally achieved her dream, but she realized it was just the beginning of something bigger.

So yes, young dreamer, follow your dreams, but remember that reaching your dreams takes time. It may take longer than you would like, but don't get discouraged.

Continue building your craft with the same love and passion that made you start, and that way, you'll always be getting better than you were before.

Julia's Magic

Not everyone will support you when you pursue your dreams; some may even try to bring you down or stand in your way. People like this can be one of your biggest challenges, but you *can* overcome them. Just ask Julia, the witch who lost her powers.

In Julia's world, witches drew their powers from the earth, water, fire, or air. She was an earth witch who loved the plants and flowers that grew around her, so she spent most of her time in the forest. However, although she tried to take care of the forest as much as she could, she noticed that some of her trees and flowers weren't blooming like they were supposed to. Many parts of the forest were growing weary and sick.

"There must be something I can do," she told herself. She tried happy spells, she tried having conversations with the plants, and she even tried singing to them. Every time, something would work a *little*, but not for the entire forest. Her fears worse as more and more plants began to die—if she didn't do something soon, she could lose her forest!

One day, the witches were hanging out and chatting. Fiona, who specialized in fire magic, mentioned a stone that could grant wishes.

"Where could I find this stone?" asked Julia.

"Well, from what my grandmother told me, it's held in the tallest mountain, just past the forest. But it can be a treacherous path. You'd have to climb the rocks, and there may even be scary creatures lurking around."

"I'll fight every creature and climb as high as I have to if it means I can get this stone and wish for the forest to be healthy!" said Julia.

"Don't be silly, Julia," said another witch. Julia turned to see her rival, Luna, laughing at her. "That stone would be put to better use if I used it to make my oceans look more beautiful."

"Well, I need it to help my forest, so *I'm* going to get that stone," Julia repeated.

"Your forest is destined to fall. Meanwhile, my oceans are eternal. You see why it makes more sense for me to use it?" she asked with a smirk.

"It's *not* destined to fall, it can even thrive! Your reasons for taking the stone are ridiculous!" she insisted.

"Only one way to see who wants the stone more. May the best witch win in the race up the mountain!" declared Luna. The two agreed that they would both race to the top of the mountain tomorrow.

Julia went to bed that night and poured herself a glass of water, just as she always did before she slept. However, for some reason, the water tasted a little different. When she woke up the next morning, she tried to speak to and control the plants around her, asking how they slept and encouraging them to grow and be healthy. However, nothing happened.

"My powers are gone!" she gasped. "Could it have been the water I drank that night?"

she wondered, scared for a moment, but she shook it off. "This is just a setback, but I'll worry about it later. What's more important is saving my forest."

She went around her house and made sure she grabbed everything she would need for her trip, then she headed out on her journey, determined to get the stone. When she got to the mountain, she saw Luna waiting for her.

"Are you ready for the race?" she asked.

"I am," Julia nodded.

"Then let's begin!" Luna declared. She summoned up a wave of water beneath her that swelled up high and lifted her up the mountain.

Julia hiked quickly up the rocky slopes, and she was pleased to find that the land was like the forest. Because of this, she knew where to step as she climbed higher and she knew which berries to eat. She knew how to make a shelter in case it rained, and she was ready to defend herself against enemies.

As she climbed higher, she nearly slipped; some of the earth was wet! To keep herself from falling, she took a thick branch from her journey and made a walking stick so that she could hold herself up across the wet areas. It was very tiring; she had to take many breaks.

The closer to the peak that Julia climbed, the more unstable the land seemed to be. Rocks crumbled down now and then, threatening her safety, and slippery patches of water and ice began appearing more and more often. After two days of this, Julia was covered in dirt and scratches from taking cover behind boulders and falling in the mud. Without the ability to talk to plant life, she had to search for her own water and food, making her journey more tedious. She could hear the predators roaming nearby, but she wasn't sure what they were. There were times when she was scared and wanted to turn and run back to her home, but when she thought of her forest turning gray and lifeless, she shook her fears away. She couldn't struggle this much only to lose. She would fight whoever she needed to save the thing she loved. She was exhausted but still determined.

Finally, she had reached the peak, and a bright green sparkle caught her eye. It was the stone! She rushed forward, but as she reached for it, a wave of water crashed into her, sending her to the ground.

She looked up to see Luna standing in front of her, her hand outstretched, almost to the stone. Julia took her cane and thrust it forward, smacking Luna's hand back and pulling the green, sparkling rock towards herself. She reached out and grabbed it out of the air, but an arm made of water reached out and wrapped itself around her hand, the cool water bubbling around her and yanking her back towards Luna.

The two were in a tug of war, but Julia was just one step ahead of Luna. As Luna shot another jet of water at her, Julia dodged it and closed the distance between them, using her cane to knock Luna's feet out from under her. Luna fumbled and fell, making her magic falter. The water hand splashed down to the ground in a puddle.

Before Luna could react, Julia held the stone high. "I wish to heal my forest!" she announced. It began to glow with a bright green light; it shone between her fingers. After only a moment, it crumbled into dust.

"No!" Luna cried, sitting up. "This can't be. I took away your powers. How could you have beaten me?"

"I don't need my magic to beat you," Julia sighed. "If you care about something enough, then you won't let the troubles get in your way," she explained.

Julia turned back and made her way back down the mountain, tired and sore. She wasn't even sure if the stone had actually worked until she returned to her forest and noticed everything was lively. The flowers had bloomed, the trees were healthy, everything was vibrant and flourishing. Julia took a seat under her favorite tree and leaned back. She had saved her forest, even without her powers.

There may be people that will stand in your way, young dreamer. There will be times where you are at a disadvantage and you may not be sure what to do. However, just because you are at a disadvantage doesn't mean you can't achieve your dream. No matter what someone takes from you, they can't take away your spirit.

The Power to Be Seen

We're coming to the end of our journey, young dreamer, but there is one more story I wish to share. There is something that many girls struggle with when they try to chase their dreams, and that struggle is with shyness. You may be too scared to chase your goals. Mila would have to overcome her shyness to follow her dream of being a singer.

Mila had always been very shy. There were many times where it was hard for her to make friends because she had trouble making conversation with other students, and it was even hard for her in class whenever she was called on to answer questions. However, Mila had a special power: she could turn invisible. It was something she was born with and could never explain. She even found it to be a curse at times; she wanted to be seen and heard, not missed entirely.

She never meant to use her invisibility, but it could be comforting, especially when she was at school. If the teacher called on her in class, she could turn invisible and later say that she had to go to the nurse. When she was in the hallways, if she spotted her crush, she could disappear before he walked past her. Once he was completely past, she would reappear, breathing a sigh of relief.

Even though it came in handy, it could be troublesome. If she got too nervous, she would vanish by accident. It would always happen when she was in front of large crowds, and she wouldn't even know until someone would try to call her name. One day, when she returned home from school, she realized she'd been invisible for most of the day! She hadn't realized how nervous she was getting. "Oh geez, I need to be more careful," she told herself.

She was in her next class when a poster for the talent show caught her eye. It would be held in four days, and Mila wanted to perform. It was her dream to become a singer, and singing in front of the school would be great practice for the future.

When she got home, she stood in front of her mirror and practiced the songs she wanted to sing. When she looked at herself, she felt confident in herself. But when she thought of the stage and all of the people watching her, she got nervous enough that she vanished without thinking, even though she was alone. She shook it off and became visible again. "Okay Mila, try again," she told herself. Again, when she watched herself in the mirror, she was very confident. But when she closed her eyes and imagined the audience, she was back to being invisible. What on earth was she going to do? The talent show was so soon! Mila continued to practice the best she could.

"Maybe I can practice by getting over smaller stuff at school," she thought.

The first thing she tried was to stay visible during class. When the teacher called on her, she was hesitant, but she tried to answer any questions the teacher had. It was very hard, but she managed to get through half of the day before she turned invisible again.

She then tried to talk to other kids in the hallway. It was felt very hard, and after talking to a few students, so she quickly hid so she wouldn't have to talk to anyone else. Her anxiety was beginning to get the best of her.

Before she knew it, the talent show was upon her. She had already signed up, though, and she was still determined to perform.

The night of the talent show, her mother put her hair in a neatly woven braid. "I'm a little surprised that you wanted to do the talent show. Nevertheless, I'm glad you're coming out of your shell," her mom said with a smile.

"Yeah, but I'm really nervous. I don't think I'm going to do well. Maybe I should back out," Mila sighed.

"You can do anything you want, and I think you will be awesome. If you want to hear it, I have a secret to get over being nervous."

“What is it?” Mila asked.

“Close your eyes and take a deep breath. A big breath in, and a big breath out. When you take a deep breath and relax, you can do wonders.”

“I don’t know if that will work,” Mila said, shaking her head.

“You don’t know unless you give it a shot,” her mother pointed out. She kissed her head.

“Thanks, mom,” Mila smiled.

Could taking deep breaths work? She wasn’t sure. But if that didn’t work, then how was she going to beat her nerves? She had tried beating the smaller things that made her nervous and that hadn’t worked, and now she was about to perform.

As she waited her turn, she watched some of the other kids on stage. Some kids were dancing, and others were juggling and twirling batons! They were doing really well, and Mila could feel herself getting discouraged. What if she didn't do well? What if they laughed at her? What if she turned invisible while she tried to sing? All of these thoughts made her so anxious that when she looked at her hands, she realized they weren't there. She was invisible again!

"And now, last but not least, let's welcome our final student, Mila!" the teacher announced. When she didn't come out, the teacher grew a little concerned. "Mila?" they called out.

Mila thought about her situation for a moment. She could run away right now and no one would see her. It would be almost too easy, and she was considering it more and more. But if she ran away now, she wouldn't face her fear. She wouldn't get used to the stage and the audience watching her.

Mila took a deep breath and shook off her invisibility, reappearing fully. She slowly stepped onto the stage and the audience cheered her on, making her feel a little more comfortable. She took a hold of the mic and took a deep breath. She shut her eyes and began to sing. She figured if she couldn't see the crowd, then maybe she could make it through without her powers taking over. As she did this, she felt herself getting lighter. She let her voice flow naturally and was beginning to enjoy the song she was singing. When it was over, she opened her eyes and the audience cheered for her.

At the end of the talent show, she got third place. But in the end, she didn't want to win the talent show. She wanted to prove to herself that she could sing in front of a crowd. She was seen, and now she was heard. She vowed to herself that she would sign up for the next talent show, no matter how nervous she got.

It's hard to get over being shy. It's something that takes time and, above all, it takes confidence. When you believe in yourself, you can do anything you set your mind to.

Epilogue

Little Dreamer, you've been on quite the journey.

Did you see how the girls in this book made their dreams come true? Now, think about what *your* dreams are. All of our dreams are different, but just like the girls you have read about, you have everything you need inside of you to achieve your goals and realize your dreams. Just like them, you have courage, strength, and unique characteristics that are yours alone, and they will help you realize your potential and create a life where all of your dreams can come true.

If you have the confidence to believe in how special you are, all of your dreams can become realities.

So tell me, Little Dreamer, what is *your* dream?

Bonuses

Our Gifts For you

Subscribe to our Newsletter and receive these free materials

Scan Me

www.specialartbooks.com/free-materials/

Stay Connected with Us

Instagram: @specialart_coloring
Facebook Group: Special Art – Kids Entertainment
Website: www.specialartbooks.com

Impressum

For questions, feedback, and suggestions:
support@specialartbooks.com

Ellen Mills, Special Art

www.specialartbooks.com

Made in the USA
Las Vegas, NV
06 July 2022